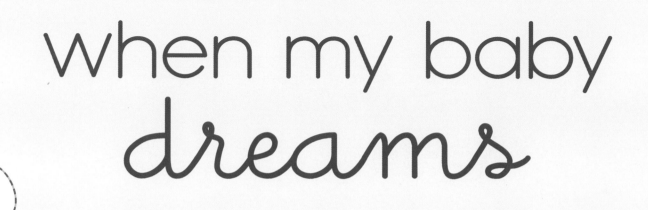

when my baby
dreams

Adele Enersen

Balzer + Bray
An Imprint of HarperCollinsPublishers

My name is Adele.
And this is my baby daughter, Mila.

After Mila was born, I was so excited, I couldn't sleep! But Mila wanted to sleep for hours and hours, so while she rested all I could do was stare at my baby and wonder . . . What was she dreaming about?

After weeks of watching Mila sleep, I finally started to see her dreams, so I decided to take pictures of them.

These are Mila's dreams.

When my baby dreams of playing with her friends . . .

she finds herself on the forest floor, picking daisies . . .

petting a little lamb . . .

and joining her playmates
on an adventure.

Even when Mila's dreaming,
she never forgets—two bears
are better than one!

When my baby dreams of being big . . .

she grows tall enough to take over the city . . .

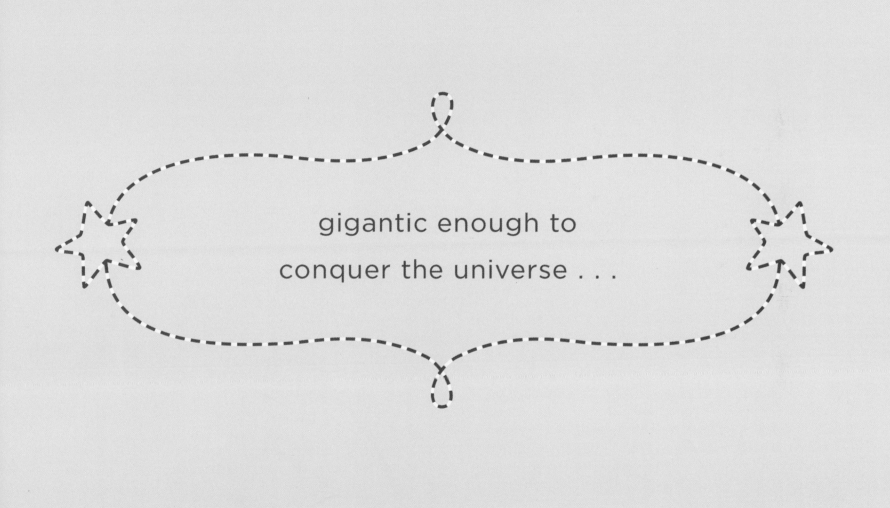

gigantic enough to

conquer the universe . . .

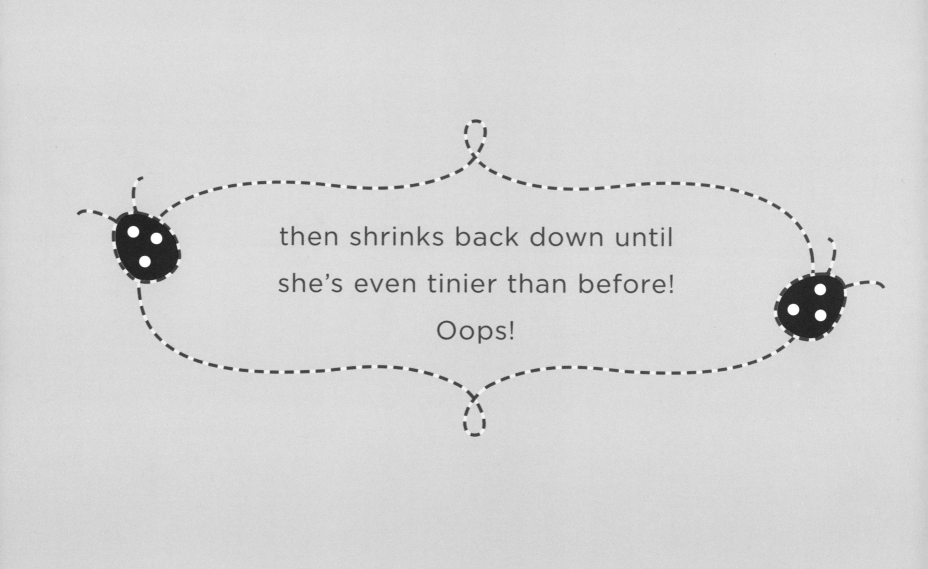

then shrinks back down until
she's even tinier than before!
Oops!

When my baby dreams of being a little bug . . .

she thinks to herself, "Today I'll be a bookworm!"

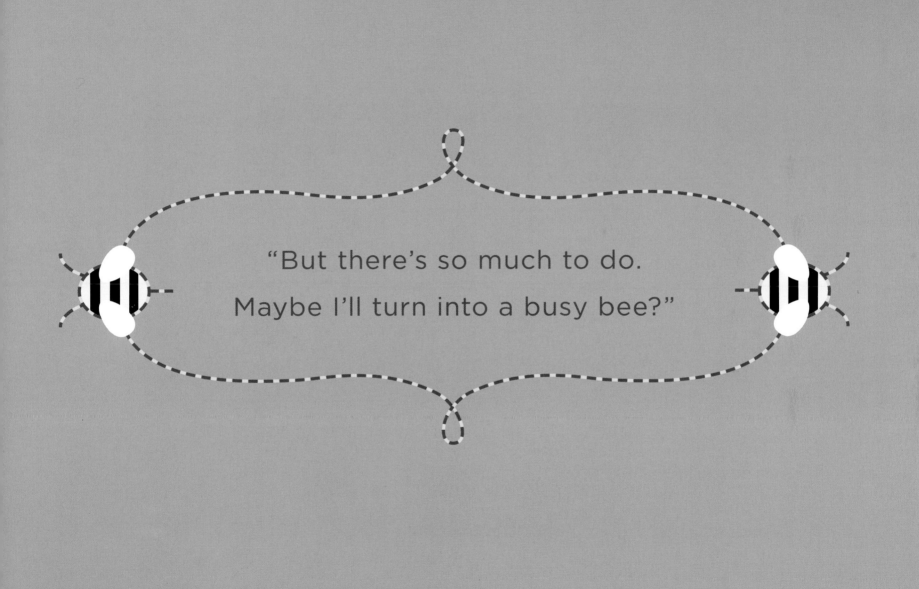

"But there's so much to do.
Maybe I'll turn into a busy bee?"

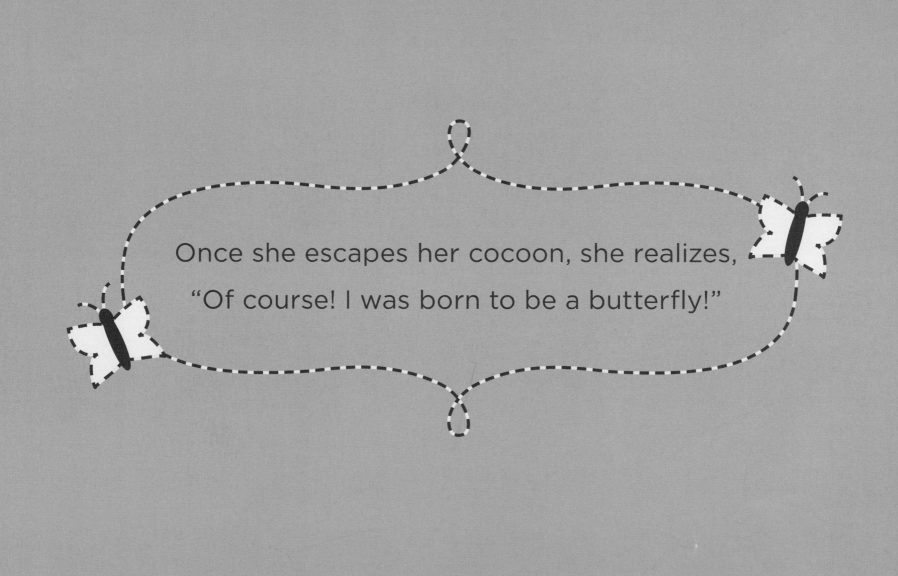

Once she escapes her cocoon, she realizes,

"Of course! I was born to be a butterfly!"

When my baby dreams of a perfectly pink world . . .

she strolls through a cotton candy park . . .

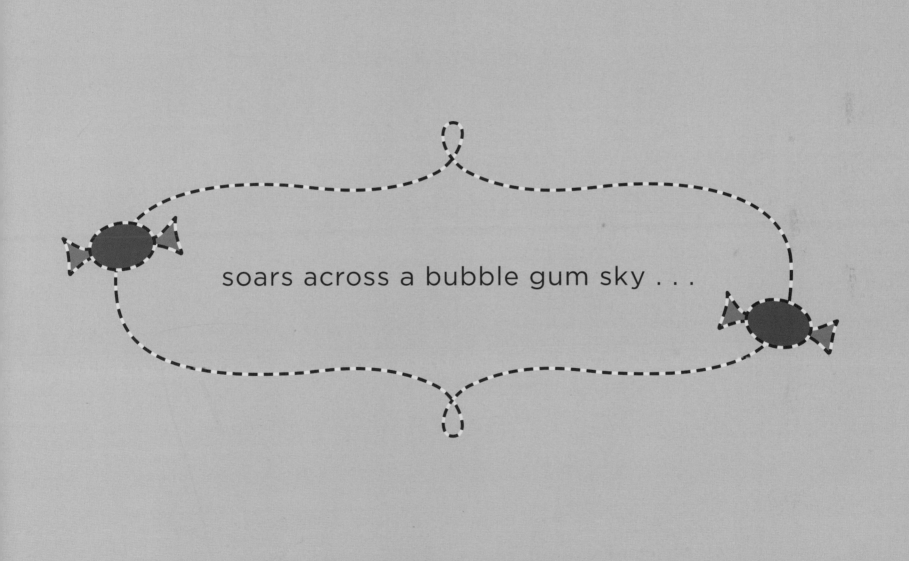

soars across a bubble gum sky . . .

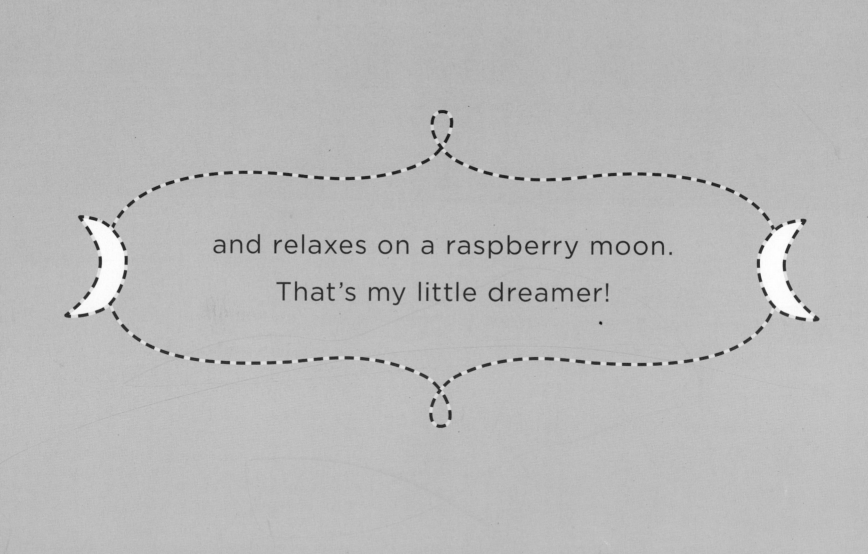

and relaxes on a raspberry moon.

That's my little dreamer!

When my baby dreams of traveling the world . . .

she starts her journey on the back of an Indian elephant . . .

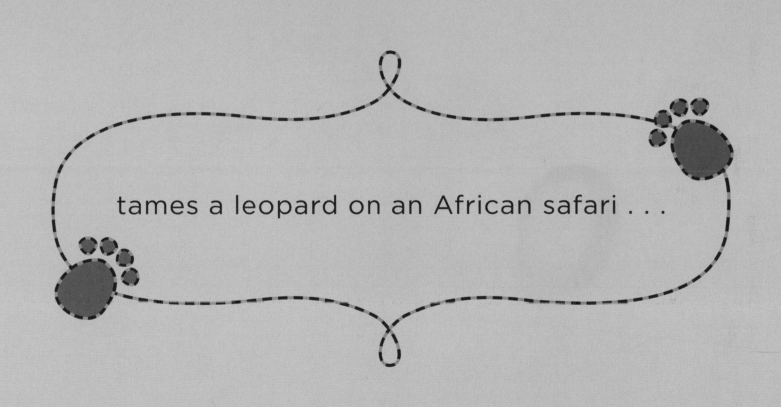

tames a leopard on an African safari . . .

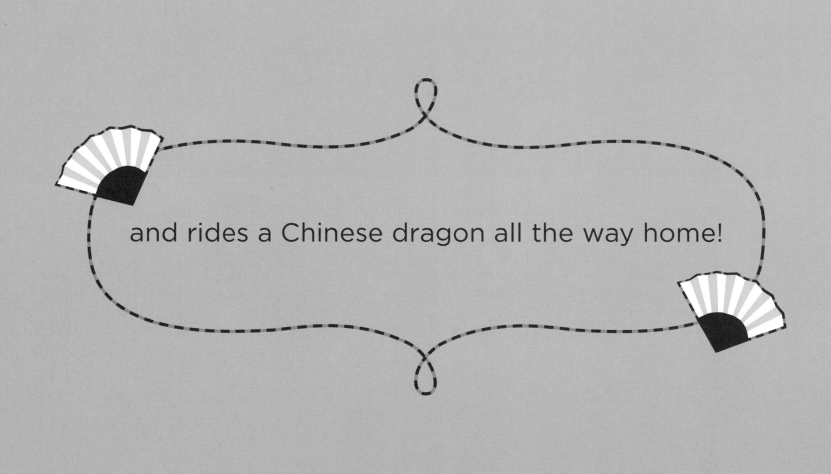

and rides a Chinese dragon all the way home!

When my baby dreams of flying . . .

she uses her birthday balloons on the way up . . .

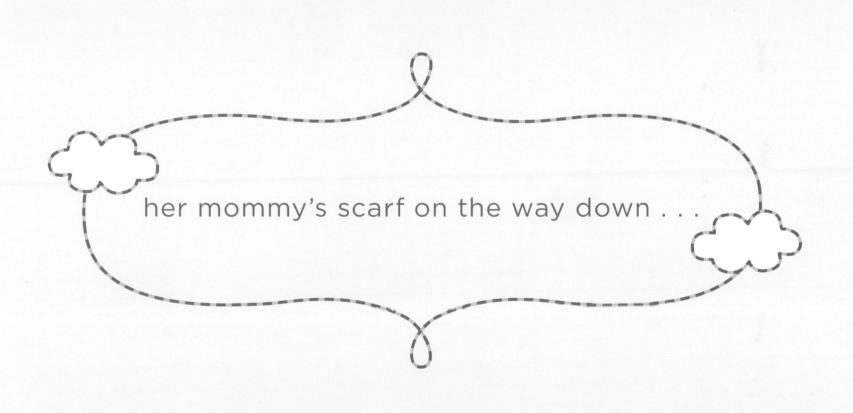

her mommy's scarf on the way down . . . .

then makes an especially soft landing.

But her socks are even softer!

When my baby dreams of living in the ocean . . .

she catches waves in the morning . . .

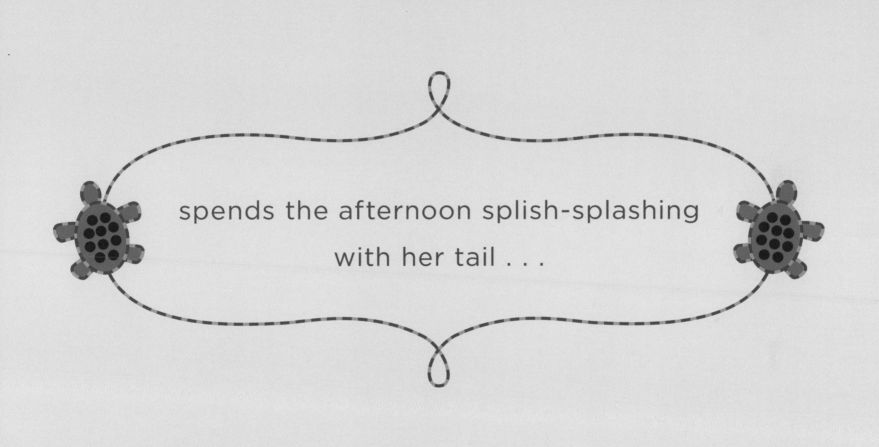

spends the afternoon splish-splashing
with her tail . . .

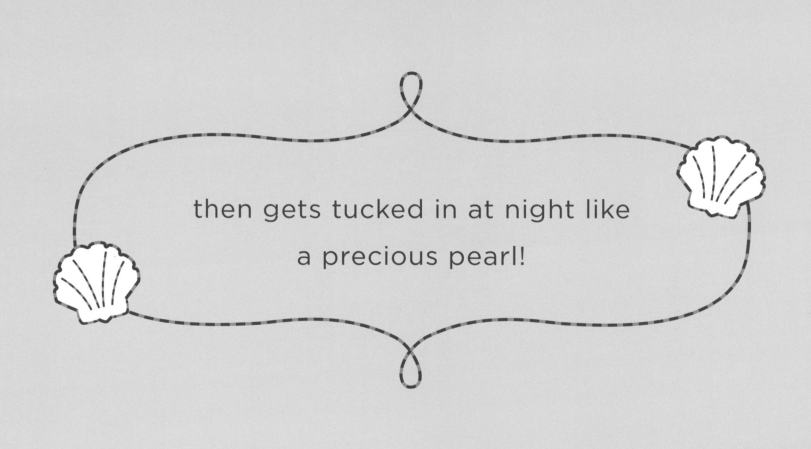

then gets tucked in at night like
a precious pearl!

When my baby finally wakes up . . .

the elephants and the butterflies and
the bubble gum skies fade away. . . .

But I'll always be there when she opens her eyes!

For Mila.
I hope all your dreams come true.

Spot illustrations by Jennifer Rozbruch

Special thanks to Dorothy Pietrewicz

Balzer + Bray is an imprint of HarperCollins Publishers.

Library of Congress Cataloging-in-Publication Data is available.
ISBN 978-0-06-207175-0

Typography by Jennifer Rozbruch

12 13 14 15 16   SCP   10 9 8 7 6 5 4 3 2 1
❖
First Edition

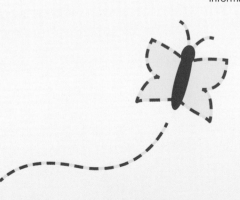